Books by Sid Fleischman

Mr. Mysterious & Company
By the Great Horn Spoon!
The Ghost in the Noonday Sun
Chancy and the Grand Rascal
Longbeard the Wizard
Jingo Django
The Wooden Cat Man
The Ghost on Saturday Night
Mr. Mysterious's Secrets of Magic
McBroom Tells a Lie
Me and the Man on the Moon-eyed Horse
McBroom and the Beanstalk
Humbug Mountain
The Hey Hey Man
McBroom and the Great Race
McBroom's Ghost
McBroom Tells the Truth

McBROOM
Tells the Truth

McBROOM
Tells the Truth

SID FLEISCHMAN

Illustrated by Walter Lorraine

An Atlantic Monthly Press Book
Little, Brown and Company
BOSTON   TORONTO

TEXT COPYRIGHT © 1966 BY SID FLEISCHMAN
ILLUSTRATIONS COPYRIGHT © 1981 BY WALTER LORRAINE
ALL RIGHTS RESERVED. NO PART OF THIS BOOK MAY BE REPRODUCED
IN ANY FORM OR BY ANY ELECTRONIC OR MECHANICAL MEANS IN-
CLUDING INFORMATION STORAGE AND RETRIEVAL SYSTEMS WITHOUT
PERMISSION IN WRITING FROM THE PUBLISHER, EXCEPT BY A REVIEWER
WHO MAY QUOTE BRIEF PASSAGES IN A REVIEW.

Library of Congress Cataloging in Publication Data

Fleischman, Sid, 1920–
  McBroom tells the truth.

  "An Atlantic Monthly Press book."
  Summary: An unfortunate land investment turns out to
be a wonderful one-acre farm.
  [1. Farms—Fiction. 2. Humorous stories]
I. Lorraine, Walter H. II. Title.
PZ7.F5992Mac 1981   [Fic]   81–1035
ISBN 0–316–28550–1   AACR2
ISBN 0–316–28552–8 (pbk.)

ATLANTIC-LITTLE, BROWN BOOKS
ARE PUBLISHED BY
LITTLE, BROWN AND COMPANY
IN ASSOCIATION WITH
THE ATLANTIC MONTHLY PRESS

HOR

Published simultaneously in Canada
by Little, Brown & Company (Canada) Limited

PRINTED IN THE UNITED STATES OF AMERICA

For Keith with happy memories

THERE HAS BEEN so much tomfool nonsense told about McBroom's wonderful one-acre farm that I had better set matters straight. I'm McBroom. Josh McBroom. I'll explain about the watermelons in a minute.

I aim to put down the facts, one after the other, the way things happened — exactly.

It began, you might say, the day we left the farm in Connecticut. We piled our youngsters and everything we owned in our old air-cooled Franklin automobile. We headed West.

To count noses, in addition to my own, there was my dear wife Melissa and our eleven red-headed, freckle-faced youngsters. Their names were Will*jill*hester*chester*peter*polly*tim*tom*mary*larry*andlittle *clarinda.*

4

It was summer, and the trees along the way were full of birdsong. We had got as far as Iowa when my dear wife Melissa made a startling discovery. We had *twelve* children along — one too many! She had just counted them again.

I slammed on the brakes and raised a cloud of dust.

"Will*jill*hester*chester*peter*polly*tim*tom*mary*larry* andlittle*clarinda*!" I shouted. "Line up!"

The youngsters tumbled out of the car. I counted noses and there were twelve. I counted again.

Twelve. It was a baffler as all the faces were familiar. Once more I made the count — but this time I caught Larry slipping around behind. He was having his nose counted twice, and the mystery was solved. The scamp! Didn't we laugh, though, and stretch our legs in the bargain.

Just then a thin, long-legged man came ambling down the road. He was so scrawny I do believe he could have hidden behind a flagpole, ears and all. He wore a tall stiff collar, a diamond stickpin in his tie, and a black hat.

"Lost, neighbor?" he asked, spitting out the pips of a green apple he was eating.

"Not a bit," said I. "We're heading West, sir. We gave up our farm — it was half rocks and the other half tree stumps. Folks tell us there's land out West and the sun shines in the winter."

The stranger pursed his lips. "You can't beat Iowa for farmland," he said.

"Maybe so," I nodded. "But I'm short of funds. Unless they're giving farms away in Iowa we'll keep a-going."

The man scratched his chin. "See here, I've got more land than I can plow. You look like nice folks. I'd like to have you for neighbors. I'll let you have

eighty acres cheap. Not a stone or a tree stump anywhere on the place. Make me an offer."

"Thank you kindly, sir," I smiled. "But I'm afraid you would laugh at me if I offered you everything in my leather purse."

"How much is that?"

"Ten dollars exactly."

"Sold!" he said.

Well, I almost choked with surprise. I thought he must be joking, but quick as a flea he was scratching out a deed on the back of an old envelope.

"Hector Jones is my name, neighbor," he said. "You can call me Heck — everyone does."

Was there ever a more kindly and generous man? He signed the deed with a flourish, and I gladly opened the clasp of my purse.

Three milky white moths flew out. They had been gnawing on the ten dollar bill all the way from Connecticut, but enough remained to buy the farm. And not a stone or tree stump on it!

Mr. Heck Jones jumped on the running board and guided us a mile up the road. My youngsters tried to amuse him along the way. Will wiggled his ears, and Jill crossed her eyes, and Chester twitched his nose like a rabbit, but I reckoned Mr. Jones wasn't used to youngsters. Hester flapped her arms like a bird, Peter whistled through his front teeth, which were missing, and Tom tried to stand on his head in the back of the car. Mr. Heck Jones ignored them all.

Finally he raised his long arm and pointed.

"There's your property, neighbor," he said.

Didn't we tumble out of the car in a hurry? We gazed with delight at our new farm. It was broad and sunny, with an oak tree on a gentle hill. There was one defect, to be sure. A boggy looking pond spread across an acre beside the road. You could lose a cow in a place like that, but we had got a bargain—no doubt about it.

"Mama," I said to my dear Melissa. "See that fine old oak on the hill? That's where we'll build our farmhouse."

"No you won't," said Mr. Heck Jones. "That oak ain't on your property."

"But, sir—"

"All that's yours is what you see under water. Not a rock or a tree stump in it, like I said."

I thought he must be having his little joke,

10

except that there wasn't a smile to be found on his face. "But, *sir!*" I said. "You clearly stated that the farm was eighty acres."

"That's right."

"That marshy pond hardly covers an acre."

"That's wrong," he said. "There are a full eighty acres—one piled on the other, like griddle cakes. I didn't say your farm was all on the surface. It's eighty acres deep, McBroom. Read the deed."

I read the deed. It was true.

"*Hee-haw! Hee-haw!*" he snorted. "I got the best of you, McBroom! Good day, neighbor."

He scurried away, laughing up his sleeve all the way home. I soon learned that Mr. Heck was always laughing up his sleeve. Folks told me that when he'd hang up his coat and go to bed, all that stored-up laughter would pour out his sleeve and keep him awake nights. But there's no truth to that.

I'll tell you about the watermelons in a minute.

WELL, there we stood gazing at our one-acre farm that wasn't good for anything but jumping into on a hot day. And the day was the hottest I could remember. The hottest on record, as it turned out. That was the day, three minutes before noon, when the cornfields all over Iowa exploded into popcorn. That's history. You must have read about that. There are pictures to prove it.

I turned to my children. "Will*jill*hester*chester*peter*polly*tim*tom*mary*larry*andlittle*clarinda*," I said. "There's always a bright side to things. That pond we bought is a mite muddy, but it's wet. Let's jump in and cool off."

That idea met with favor and we were soon in our

swimming togs. I gave the signal, and we took a running jump. At that moment such a dry spell struck that we landed in an acre of dry earth. The pond had evaporated. It was very surprising.

My boys had jumped in head first and there was nothing to be seen of them but their legs kicking in the air. I had to pluck them out of the earth like carrots. Some of my girls were still holding their noses. Of course, they were sorely disappointed to have that swimming hole pulled out from under them.

But the moment I ran the topsoil through my fingers, my farmer's heart skipped a beat. That pond bottom felt as soft and rich as black silk. "My dear Melissa!" I called. "Come look! This topsoil is so rich it ought to be kept in a bank."

I was in a sudden fever of excitement. That glorious topsoil seemed to cry out for seed. My dear Melissa had a sack of dried beans along, and I sent Will and Chester to fetch it. I saw no need to bother plowing the field. I directed Polly to draw a straight furrow with a stick and Tim to follow her, poking holes in the ground. Then I came along. I dropped a bean in each hole and stamped on it with my heel.

Well, I had hardly gone a couple of yards when something green and leafy tangled my foot. I looked behind me. There was a beanstalk traveling along in a hurry and looking for a pole to climb on.

"Glory be!" I exclaimed. That soil was *rich!* The stalks were spreading out all over. I had to rush along to keep ahead of them.

By the time I got to the end of the furrow the first stalks had blossomed, and the pods had formed, and they were ready for picking.

You can imagine our excitement. Will's ears wiggled. Jill's eyes crossed. Chester's nose twitched. Hester's arms flapped. Peter's missing front teeth whistled. And Tom stood on his head.

"Will*jill*hester*chester*peter*polly*tim*tom*mary*larry*andlittle*clarinda*," I shouted. "Harvest them beans!"

Within an hour we had planted and harvested

19

that entire crop of beans. But was it hot working in the sun! I sent Larry to find a good acorn along the road. We planted it, but it didn't grow near as fast as I had expected. We had to wait an entire three hours for a shade tree.

We made camp under our oak tree, and the next day we drove to Barnsville with our crop of beans. I traded it for various seeds — carrot and beet and cabbage and other items. The storekeeper found a few kernels of corn that hadn't popped, at the very bottom of the bin.

But we found out that corn was positively dangerous to plant. The stalk shot up so fast it would skin your nose.

Of course, there was a secret to that topsoil. A government man came out and made a study of the matter. He said there had once been a huge lake in that part of Iowa. It had taken thousands of years to shrink up to our pond, as you can imagine. The lake fish must have got packed in worse than sardines. There's nothing like fish to put nitrogen in the soil. That's a scientific fact. Nitrogen makes things grow to beat all. And we did occasionally turn up a fish bone.

It wasn't long before Mr. Heck Jones came around to pay us a neighborly call. He was eating a raw turnip. When he saw the way we were planting and harvesting cabbage his eyes popped out of his head. It almost cost him his eyesight.

He scurried away, muttering to himself.

"My dear Melissa," I said. "That man is up to mischief."

Folks in town had told me that Mr. Heck Jones had the worst farmland in Iowa. He couldn't give it away. Tornado winds had carried off his topsoil and left the hardpan right on top. He had to plow it with wedges and a sledge hammer. One day we heard a lot of booming on the other side of the hill, and my youngsters went up to see what was happening. It turned out he was planting seeds with a shotgun.

Meanwhile, we went about our business on the farm. I don't mind saying that before long we were

showing a handsome profit. Back in Connecticut
we had been lucky to harvest one crop a year. Now
we were planting and harvesting three, four crops
a *day*.

But there were things we had to be careful about.
Weeds, for one thing. My youngsters took turns
standing weed guard. The instant a weed popped
out of the ground, they'd race to it and hoe it to
death. You can imagine what would happen if weeds
ever got going in rich soil like ours.

We also had to be careful about planting time. Once we planted lettuce just before my dear Melissa rang the noon bell for dinner. While we ate, the lettuce headed up and went to seed. We lost the whole crop.

One day back came Mr. Heck Jones with a grin on his face. He had figured out a loophole in the deed that made the farm ours.

"*Hee-haw!*" he laughed. He was munching a

radish. "I got the best of you now, Neighbor McBroom. The deed says you were to pay me *everything* in your purse, and you *didn't.*"

"On the contrary, sir," I answered. "Ten dollars. There wasn't another cent in my purse."

"There were *moths* in the purse. I seen 'em flutter out. Three milky white moths, McBroom. I want three moths by three o'clock this afternoon, or I aim to take back the farm. *Hee-haw!*"

And off he went, laughing up his sleeve.

Mama was just ringing the noon bell so we didn't have much time. Confound that man! But he did have his legal point.

"Willjillhesterchesterpeterpollytimtommarylarryandlittle clarinda!" I said. "We've got to catch three milky white moths! Hurry!"

We hurried in all directions. But moths are next to impossible to locate in the daytime. Try it yourself. Each of us came back empty-handed.

My dear Melissa began to cry, for we were sure to lose our farm. I don't mind telling you that things looked dark. Dark! That was it! I sent the youngsters running down the road to a lonely old pine tree and told them to rush back with a bushel of pine cones.

Didn't we get busy though! We planted a pine cone every three feet. They began to grow. We stood around anxiously, and I kept looking at my pocket watch. I'll tell you about the watermelons in a moment.

Sure enough, by ten minutes to three, those cones had grown into a thick pine forest.

It was dark inside, too! Not a ray of sunlight slipped through the green pine boughs. Deep in the forest I lit a lantern. Hardly a minute passed before

I was surrounded by milky white moths—they thought it was night. I caught three on the wing and rushed out of the forest.

There stood Mr. Heck Jones waiting with the sheriff to foreclose.

"*Hee-haw! Hee-haw!*" old Heck laughed. He was eating a quince apple. "It's nigh onto three o'clock, and you can't catch moths in the daytime. The farm is mine!"

"Not so fast, Neighbor Jones," said I, with my hands cupped together. "Here are the three moths.

Now, skedaddle, sir, before your feet take root and poison ivy grows out of your ears!"

He scurried away, muttering to himself.

"My dear Melissa," I said. "That man is up to mischief. He'll be back."

It took a good bit of work to clear the timber, I'll tell you. We had some of the pine milled and built ourselves a house on the corner of the farm. What was left we gave away to our neighbors. We were weeks blasting the roots out of the ground.

But I don't want you to think there was nothing but work on our farm. Some crops we grew just for the fun of it. Take pumpkins. The vines grew so fast we could hardly catch the pumpkins. It was something to see. The youngsters used to wear themselves out running after those pumpkins. Sometimes they'd have pumpkin races.

Sunday afternoons, just for the sport of it, the older boys would plant a pumpkin seed and try to catch a ride. It wasn't easy. You had to grab hold the

instant the blossom dropped off and the pumpkin began to swell. Whoosh! It would yank you off your feet and take you whizzing over the farm until it wore itself out. Sometimes they'd use banana squash, which was faster.

And the girls learned to ride corn stalks like pogo sticks. It was just a matter of standing over the kernel as the stalk came busting up through the ground. It was good for quite a bounce.

We'd see Mr. Heck Jones standing on the hill in the distance, watching. He wasn't going to rest until he had pried us off our land.

Then, late one night, I was awakened by a hee-hawing outside the house. I went to the window and saw old Heck in the moonlight. He was cackling and chuckling and heeing and hawing and sprinkling seed every which way.

I pulled off my sleeping cap and rushed outside.

"What mischief are you up to, Neighbor Jones!" I shouted.

35

"*Hee-haw!*" he answered, and scurried away, laughing up his sleeve.

I had a sleepless night, as you can imagine. The next morning, as soon as the sun came up, that farm of ours broke out in weeds. You never saw such weeds! They heaved out of the ground and tumbled madly over each other — chickweed and milkweed, thistles and wild morning glory. In no time at all the weeds were in a tangle several feet thick and still rising.

We had a fight on our hands, I tell you! "Willjillhesterchesterpeterpollytimtommarylarryand-littleclarinda!" I shouted. "There's work to do!"

We started hoeing and hacking away. For every weed we uprooted, another reseeded itself. We were a solid month battling those weeds. If our neighbors hadn't pitched in to help, we'd still be there burning weeds.

The day finally came when the farm was cleared and up popped old Heck Jones. He was eating a big slice of watermelon. That's what I was going to tell you about.

"Howdy, Neighbor McBroom," he said. "I came to say goodbye."

"Are you leaving, sir?" I asked.

"No, but *you* are."

I looked him squarely in the eye. "And if I don't, sir?"

"Why, *hee-haw*, McBroom! There's heaps more of weed seed where that came from!"

My dander was up. I rolled back my sleeves, meaning to give him a whipping he wouldn't forget. But what happened next saved me the bother.

As my youngsters gathered around, Mr. Heck

Jones made the mistake of spitting out a mouthful of watermelon seeds.

Things did happen fast!

Before I had quite realized what he had done, a watermelon vine whipped up around old Heck's scrawny legs and jerked him off his feet. He went whizzing every which way over the farm. Water-

melon seeds were flying. Soon he came zipping back and collided with a pumpkin left over from Sunday. In no time watermelons and pumpkins went galloping all over the place, and they were knocking him about something wild. He streaked here and there. Melons crashed and exploded. Old Heck was so covered with melon pulp he looked like he had been shot out of a ketchup bottle.

It was something to see. Will stood there wiggling his ears. Jill crossed her eyes. Chester twitched his nose. Hester flapper her arms like a bird. Peter whistled through his front teeth, which had grown in. Tom stood on his head. And little Clarinda took her first step.

By then the watermelons and pumpkins began to play themselves out. I figured Mr. Heck Jones would like to get home as fast as possible. So I asked Larry to fetch me the seed of a large banana squash.

"*Hee-haw!* Neighbor Jones," I said, and pitched the seed at his feet. I hardly had time to say goodbye before the vine had him. A long banana squash gave him a fast ride all the way home. I wish you could have been there to see it. He never came back.

That's the entire truth of the matter. Anything else you hear about McBroom's wonderful one-acre farm is an outright fib.